KU-617-104

Thumbelina

TOWER HAMLETS LIBRARIES	
SOURCE BfS	PRICE £ 3.99
02 Feb 2005	
LOCN. CUB	CLASS JF
ACC. No. C1313205	

TOWER
HAMLETS
LIBRARIES

There was once a woman who wanted a small child, but didn't know where to get one. So she went to a witch for help.

"A little child?" said the witch. "That's easy. Here's a magic seed from the warm countries. Plant it in a flower pot and see what happens!"

4

The woman thanked the witch, paid her with a piece of silver and went home to plant the magic seed. As soon as it touched the soil, the seed grew into a tulip, whose flower opened with a pop. In the middle of the flower sat a tiny girl.

"Why, the pretty little thing is hardly as big as my thumb!" cried the woman. "I'm going to call her Thumbelina."

The woman made Thumbelina a bed from a walnut shell. Instead of going out, Thumbelina played on the kitchen table. Her favourite game was sailing across a bowl of water in a boat made from a tulip leaf. As she sailed, she sang in a high, sweet voice.

One night, an old, damp toad got in through an open window and hopped down on to the kitchen table. "Just the wife for my son!" the toad declared when she saw Thumbelina sleeping in her tiny bed.

The toad picked up the walnut shell and hopped out through the window into the garden.

At the bottom of the garden there was a stream with muddy banks and that was where the old toad lived with her son. He was even damper and uglier than his mother.

When he saw the pretty little girl asleep in the walnut shell, all he could say was "Ribbik! Ribbik!"

"Not so loud!" whispered the old toad. "If you wake her up, she'll run away. We'll put her on a water-lily leaf in the middle of the stream so she won't be able to escape. Then we can clear out the best room for the wedding."

In the morning when she woke, Thumbelina was startled to find herself on a big green leaf in the middle of a stream. She was even more startled when the toads appeared.

"We've come to move your bed into the best room, my dear," said the old toad. "Meet your husband. I'm sure you'll both live happily ever after."

"Ribbik! Ribbik!" croaked her son.

As the toads swam back to the bank, Thumbelina cried so loudly that the fish in the stream poked their heads out of the water to ask what the matter was. When Thumbelina told them, they all agreed it was a shame for a pretty girl like her to marry an ugly toad. They bit through the stalk of Thumbelina's lily leaf and it floated away downstream.

Thumbelina drifted past fields and towns for hours, until she was spotted by a big beetle that was flying past. The beetle grabbed her round the waist and flew her up into a tree.

"You're so pretty. I'm going to have a dinner party to show you off to my friends!" the beetle declared.

But when the other beetles arrived at the party, they said unkind things about Thumbelina.

"She's *so* ugly!"

"She's only got two legs!"

"She has no feelers at all!"

The beetle who had carried off Thumbelina was so disappointed when he heard his friends talking in this way that he ended up believing them. He flew Thumbelina down to the foot of the tree.

"Off you go!" he said. "You're far too ugly to live with me!"

All that summer, Thumbelina lived alone in the wood. She ate the sweet parts of flowers and drank the morning dew, while birds sang to her from the trees.

Summer turned to autumn and then winter came. Thumbelina shivered with cold. The birds who had sung to her flew away; the trees shed their leaves and the flowers shrivelled up. It snowed, and flakes landed on Thumbelina as heavily as wet blankets.

She left the wood to search for a warmer place to stay.

At the edge of the wood was a field of stubble. As Thumbelina struggled across it, she stumbled into the entrance to a field mouse's home, snug and cosy underground.

"Please could you spare me some food?" begged Thumbelina. "I haven't eaten anything for two days."

"You poor child!" said the kind-hearted field mouse. "Come in and get warm! I've got plenty of food in my pantry, so you can stay all winter, so long as you keep my house tidy and sing to me. I like a good tune."

So Thumbelina kept house and sang for the field mouse and the time passed happily.

"We're going to have a visitor," the field mouse told Thumbelina one day. "A neighbour of mine visits me quite often. He wears such a fine black velvet coat that I'm sure he's very rich. He'd make a fine husband for you, my dear!

He's blind and it's a shame he can't see how pretty you are. You must sing him your loveliest songs."

The neighbour was a mole and Thumbelina didn't like him. He talked about how much he hated the sun and flowers, even though he had never seen them. When Thumbelina sang, the mole fell in love with her at once.

"Dear field mouse," he said, "perhaps you and your young friend would like to take a stroll along the new tunnel I've dug from my house to yours. There's a dead bird in it. It fell in when the weather turned cold – stupid thing!"

The mole led the way along the dark tunnel. When he came to the place where the bird lay, he pushed his nose against the ceiling and made a hole for the sun to shine through.

Thumbelina saw that the bird was a swallow. She felt sorry for it.

"Birds are such nasty creatures!" said the mole.

"I couldn't agree more," said the field mouse. "Just because they can fly, they think they're better than the rest of us."

"Poor bird!" thought Thumbelina. "I wonder if you sang for me in the summer?"

When the mole and the field mouse
turned their backs, Thumbelina stroked
the bird's feathers. To her surprise, she
felt the swallow's heart beating.

"Why, he's not dead at all!" she
whispered. "The cold has made him fall
into a deep sleep. If I could make him
warm, he might wake up."

She said nothing to the field mouse
and the mole because they hated the
swallow.

The mole blocked up the hole in the ceiling and they continued to walk.

That night, Thumbelina crept out with some cotton wool to cover the bird.

The next night, when she went to see him again, his eyes were open. She took him water in an acorn cup and when he had drunk it, he was able to speak to her.

"Thank you, pretty child," he said.
"I hurt my wing on a thorn bush
and I couldn't fly away with the other
swallows at the end of the summer. As
soon as I get my strength back, I'll fly
out in the warm sunshine."

"But it's not warm," said Thumbelina.
"You must wait until the spring."
All through the winter,
Thumbelina visited
the swallow and
took care of him.
As soon as spring
warmed the earth, she
opened the hole in the ceiling
and let the bright sunshine pour in.

"Come with me," said the swallow,
for he had grown fond of his little nurse.

"You can sit on my back and I'll fly you far away from this dark place."

"I can't," said Thumbelina sadly. "The field mouse has been so kind, I don't want to hurt her feelings."

"Goodbye, then," said the swallow and he flew off into the sunshine.

The field mouse told Thumbelina that there was a lot of work to be done.

"You'll soon be married to the mole, and you haven't got a wedding dress!" she said.

The mole hired four spiders to weave and Thumbelina spent every day sewing. Though she said nothing, she was very sad. She knew that once

she married the mole, she would never
see the sky, or sunshine, or flowers
again. When she tried to explain how
she felt, the field mouse snapped at her.

"You ought to be grateful! You'll live
in luxury! Now your dress is finished,
you can be married
tomorrow, so stop
all this nonsense
at once!"

The next morning, Thumbelina stole
outside to take a last look at the sun.
It was late summer and the field was
as stubbly as when she had first seen it.

Thumbelina lifted up
her arms to say
goodbye to the
sun, and a dark
shape flashed
past her. It was
the swallow.

Thumbelina was so glad to see him
that all the sadness she felt about
marrying the mole turned into tears
that ran down her face.

"Come with me to the warm
countries!" said the swallow. "It's
always summer there! It's the place

where magic flowers grow! You saved
me from death, let me save you from
a life of darkness!"

"Yes, I'll go with you," said
Thumbelina.

She climbed on to the swallow's back
and he flew up high, over forests and
seas and high mountains. When the air
grew cold, Thumbelina nestled under
the swallow's feathers and stayed warm.

At last they came to the warm countries, where there were orange and lemon trees, and lovely flowers that Thumbelina had never seen before. The further on the swallow flew, the more beautiful everything became. He showed her a ruined palace beside a blue lake.

"That's where I make my nest," he said. "But I'm sure you would rather live in one of those big flowers over there."

"Oh, yes please!" cried Thumbelina.

The swallow swooped down and set Thumbelina on a leaf next to a huge white flower.

And there, in the middle of the flower, was a handsome young man, no bigger than Thumbelina herself. He wore a golden crown.

"Who are you?" Thumbelina gasped.

"I'm the prince of the flower," said the young man. "Every flower in this place has a prince or princess inside it, but I've never seen a princess as pretty as you."

Thumbelina blushed as the young man took off his crown and placed it on her head.

"Will you be my wife?" he asked her.

Thumbelina said yes at once, for the young prince was far more handsome than the toad's son and the mole.

She had a fine wedding, and was given many presents by the flower princes and princesses, and was happier than she had ever been in her life.

And that's a proper ending to a story!

The Tin Soldier

"Tin soldiers!" shouted the little boy, as he opened his birthday present.

Carefully, he took the soldiers out of their box and lined them up in a parade across the table.

There were twenty-five soldiers,
wearing red and blue uniforms,
standing smartly to attention with
rifles leaning on their shoulders. They
all looked the same – except one. He
had been made last, when the tin was
running out, and he only had one leg;
even so, he stood as straight as the rest.
This is what happened to him.

There were other toys on the table.
The most spectacular was a paper
castle. In front of the castle, paper trees
stood on the banks of a lake made
from a small mirror. In the lake, wax
swans swam on top of their reflections.

It all looked lovely, and loveliest of all was a paper dancer, who stood in the castle's open door.

Her dress was white, and round her shoulders was a scarf of blue ribbon. On the scarf was a sparkling sequin, as big as her face. The dancer's arms were stretched out and one of her legs was lifted up so high that the soldier couldn't see it.

"Why, she's only got one leg, like me!" he thought. "What a perfect wife she would make...only...she lives in a castle, while I have to share a box with twenty-four other soldiers. That's no place for a lady! Oh, if only I could speak to her!"

The soldier hid himself behind a music box and gazed at the dancer, who balanced on tiptoe so beautifully.

That night, the other soldiers were packed away into their box. As soon as the people of the house were in bed asleep, the toys started to chatter and play. The crayons scribbled in the colouring books, the teddy bear turned somersaults. The tin soldiers rattled their box, trying to lift the lid so they could join in. The only toys who kept still were the dancer and the soldier, who stood firm on his one leg and stared at her without blinking.

Midnight chimed, the lid of the music box flew open and out sprang a small, ugly troll.

"Tin soldier!" the troll snapped. "Keep your eyes off that dancer!"

The soldier ignored him.

"All right – just you wait until tomorrow!" said the troll.

In the morning, when the children were up, the tin soldier was put on the window sill. Maybe it was a breeze and maybe it was troll-magic, but the

window blew open and the soldier
tumbled down into the street. He
landed on his helmet, with his one leg
in the air and his rifle stuck in a crack
in the pavement. The children hurried
outside, but though they almost trod on
the soldier, they didn't find him.

It began to pour down with rain.
Two boys scampered up the street,
holding a newspaper over their heads
to keep dry.

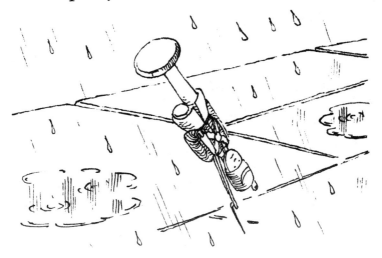

"Here's a tin soldier!" cried one.
"Let's turn him into a sailor."

They made a newspaper boat, put the soldier inside and floated him off along the gutter. It was a bumpy ride, but no matter how the boat rocked and shook and twirled, the brave tin soldier stood to attention and kept his gun on his shoulder.

"I bet this is troll's work!" thought the soldier. "Where am I off to? Oh, if the dancer were with me now, I wouldn't care where I was going!"

Up popped a water rat, who lived in the drain.

"Show me your passport!" it hissed. The soldier stayed quiet and held his rifle even tighter. The boat raced on.

"Come back!" the rat shouted. "You can't go down the drains without having your passport stamped!"

The boat plunged into the drain, where the water crashed and roared like a waterfall. The drain flowed out into a deep canal. The soldier was spun round and round, but he kept as straight as he could, even when the boat began to sink.

"I'll never see the paper dancer again!" he thought, as the water rose over his head.

Just then, everything went dark, because a big, greedy fish swallowed him up.

"It's dark and narrow in here!" thought the soldier. "But I must be brave and stand firm!"

The fish jumped and jiggled and wiggled about and then all was quiet and still. There was a sudden flash of light and a voice shouted, "The tin soldier!" The fish had been caught, sold at market and carried to a kitchen, where a cook had cut it open with a long knife. The cook picked up the soldier and went to show everybody the strange thing the fish had swallowed.

The soldier was placed on a table and – it's a funny old world! – he found himself in the same room as before! There was the little boy, there was the castle and there was the dancer, still on tiptoe. The soldier gazed at her, but said nothing.

Maybe it was naughtiness, or maybe it was the troll again, but the little boy suddenly grabbed the tin soldier and threw him into the fire. The soldier kept straight as long as he could, but he could feel that he was slowly melting.

He gazed at the dancer and she gazed back at him.

A door slammed somewhere and a draught lifted the dancer into the air. She flew straight to the soldier and stood at his side for a moment before she burst into flames and vanished.

When the fireplace was cleared
out the following morning, all that
was left of the dancer was her sequin,
burned black.

And the soldier? He had melted
down into a tiny lump of tin, shaped
like a heart.

TOWER
HAMLET'
LIBRAR'